HURRAY for the FOURTH of JULY

Wendy Watson

Clarion Books · New York

For Peter and Tom,
with flourishes

Calligraphy on jacket and title page by Paul Shaw.
Clarion Books
a Houghton Mifflin Company imprint
215 Park Avenue South, New York, NY 10003
Text and illustrations copyright © 1992 by Wendy Watson
Printed in the U.S.A.

Library of Congress Cataloging-in-Publication Data
Watson, Wendy.
Hurray for the Fourth of July / by Wendy Watson.
p.   cm.
Summary: A small-town family celebrates the Fourth of July by
attending a parade, having a picnic, and watching fireworks.
Interspersed throughout the pages are patriotic songs and
traditional rhymes.
ISBN 0-395-53627-8
[1. Fourth of July—Fiction.]   I. Title.
PZ7.W332Hu   1992
[E]—dc20   91-23892
                              CIP   AC

HOR   10   9   8   7   6   5   4   3   2   1

O BEAUTIFUL FOR SPACIOUS SKIES,
FOR AMBER WAVES OF GRAIN,
FOR PURPLE MOUNTAIN MAJESTIES
ABOVE THE FRUITED PLAIN!
AMERICA! AMERICA!
GOD SHED HIS GRACE ON THEE!
AND CROWN THY GOOD WITH BROTHERHOOD
FROM SEA TO SHINING SEA!

Crack! Pop! Snap!
Wake up, everybody—
today is the Fourth of July.
It's America's birthday!

Everything is red, white, and blue,
even breakfast.

Are those the drums?
Come on—
the parade is about to begin.

Boom-dee-dah-boom!
Boom-dee-dah-boom!
The band is loud.
Our feet step high and fast,
left, right, left, right.
Hey, kitty—come back!

YANKEE DOODLE WENT TO TOWN,
RIDING ON A PONY,
HE STUCK A FEATHER IN HIS CAP,
AND CALLED IT MACARONI.

YANKEE DOODLE, KEEP IT UP,
YANKEE DOODLE DANDY,
MIND THE MUSIC AND THE STEP,
AND WITH THE GIRLS BE HANDY.

TWO'S A COUPLE,
THREE'S A CROWD;
FOUR ON THE SIDEWALK
IS NEVER ALLOWED.

We get a prize!

There are lots of speeches.

ROOT BEER SODA, LEMONADE POP;
TAKE A LITTLE SIP, AND DO A LITTLE HOP.

I SCREAM,
YOU SCREAM,
WE ALL SCREAM
FOR ICE CREAM.

THE BOY STOOD ON THE BURNING DECK,
EATING PEANUTS BY THE PECK.
A GIRL CAME BY ALL DRESSED IN BLUE,
AND SAID, I GUESS I'LL HAVE SOME TOO.

At last it's time for lunch.
We buy hot dogs and ice cream cones,
lemonade and peanuts,
cotton candy and soda and pretzels.

Now
there are
games and races.
Some people play baseball.

FIRE ON THE MOUNTAIN,
RUN, BOYS, RUN;
THE CAT'S IN THE CREAMPOT,
RUN, GIRLS, RUN!

Dad chases the greased pig. Come on, Dad—you can do it!

The sun is hot.
We go for a swim.

Here's doggie!
He swims, too.

VIRGINIA HAD A BABY;
SHE NAMED IT TINY TIM.
SHE PUT IT IN THE BATHTUB
TO TEACH IT HOW TO SWIM.
IT FLOATED UP THE RIVER,
IT FLOATED DOWN THE LAKE;
NOW VIRGINIA'S BABY
HAS THE STOMACH ACHE.

Our legs are tired.
We go back home.
The house is cool and quiet.
We're very sleepy.

When we wake up, the picnic is ready.
Dad carries the blankets.
The whole town is coming!
We find a good place to sit.

JO, JO,
BROKE HER TOE,
RIDING ON A BUFFALO.

MY SON JOHN IS A NICE OLD MAN,
WASHED HIS FACE IN A FRYING PAN,
COMBED HIS HAIR WITH A WAGON WHEEL,
AND DANCED WITH THE TOOTHACHE IN HIS HEEL.

WHERE WAS MOSES WHEN THE LIGHT WENT OUT?
DOWN IN THE CELLAR WITH HIS SHIRT-TAIL OUT.

MY MOTHER AND YOUR MOTHER LIVE ACROSS THE WAY;
EVERY NIGHT THEY HAVE A FIGHT, AND THIS IS WHAT THEY SAY:
ICKA BACKA, SODA CRACKER, ICKA BACKA BOO;
ICKA BACKA, SODA CRACKER, OUT GOES YOU!

TEACHER, TEACHER, MADE A MISTAKE —
SHE SAT DOWN ON A CHOCOLATE CAKE.
THE CAKE WAS SOFT,
TEACHER FELL OFF —
TEACHER, TEACHER, MADE A MISTAKE!

Mom serves fried chicken and potato salad.
We light the birthday cake.
Ouch! Even the mosquitoes are here.
Look—they're going to start the fireworks!

Bang! BOOM!

BOOM!

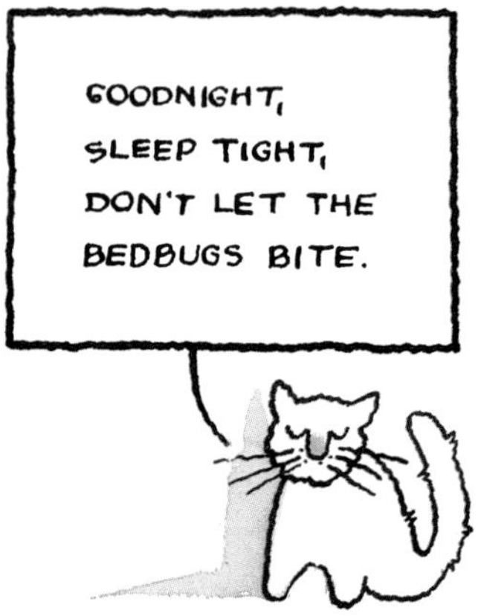
GOODNIGHT,
SLEEP TIGHT,
DON'T LET THE
BEDBUGS BITE.